BOOKS

If

BOOKBUS

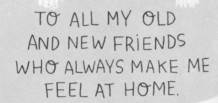

TO ALL MY OLD
AND NEW FRIENDS
WHO ALWAYS MAKE ME
FEEL AT HOME.

First published 2014 by
Macmillan Children's Books
a division of Macmillan Publishers Limited
20 New Wharf Road, London N1 9RR
Basingstoke and Oxford
Associated companies throughout the world
www.panmacmillan.com

ISBN: 978-1-4472-0650-7

Text and illustrations copyright
© Marta Altés 2014
Moral rights asserted.
Thanks to my editor Emily Ford
and designer Sharon King-Chai

1 3 5 7 9 8 6 4 2

A CIP catalogue record for this book is
available from the British Library.

Printed in China.

marta altés

MY NEW HOME

MACMILLAN CHILDREN'S BOOKS

We've just moved house

and I feel so far from home.

I was happy in my old house.

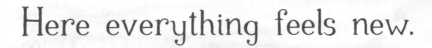

Here everything feels new.

I don't really like it.

New can be scary . . .

. . . and a little bit lonely.

Dad says
not to worry.

He says that when I least expect it . . .

I'll find new adventures.

And adventures
make loneliness
disappear . . .

I still miss my old friends.

But sometimes it feels
like they are here.

When I moved house
I felt far from home.

Here everything feels new.

But new can be exciting!

I think I'm very lucky . . .

. . . and I feel at
home again.